D1246490

THE GREATEST
SHEEP
IN HISTORY

DELETE

Extraordinary Ernie
& Marvelous Maud

THE GREATEST
SHEEP
IN HISTORY

Frances Watts
Illustrated by Judy Watson

Eerdmans Books for Young Readers

Grand Rapids, Michigan / Cambridge, U.K.

Text © 2009 Frances Watts
Illustrations © 2009 Judy Watson

First published 2009 in Australia by
Australian Broadcasting Corporation

This edition published 2011 in the United States of America by
Eerdmans Books for Young Readers
an imprint of Wm. B. Eerdmans Publishing Co.

Wm. B. Eerdmans Publishing Co.
2140 Oak Industrial Dr. NE, Grand Rapids, Michigan 49505
P.O. Box 163, Cambridge CB3 9PU U.K.

www.eerdmans.com/youngreaders

Manufactured at Versa Press, East Peoria, Illinois, USA,
in December 2010; first printing

11 12 13 14 15 16 17   7 6 5 4 3 2 1

Library of Congress Cataloging-in-Publication Data

For Valiant Christa and Courageous Cath,
and to Jittery Judy for her services
to superheroes.

— F.W.

For Bel and Sass.

— J.W.

ONE

Ernie Eggers hurried along Main Street on Thursday afternoon, his bright green cape billowing behind him. When he heard the clock on Baxter town hall strike four, he gave a sigh of relief. Phew! He'd been worried that he'd be late.

Farther up the street, he could see his sidekick, Maud, already waiting outside number 32, the headquarters of the Superheroes Society (Baxter Branch). When Ernie had first won the competition to become a trainee superhero, he'd been disappointed to learn that his sidekick was a sheep. But that was before he got to know Maud.

Now that they had been working together for several months, patrolling Baxter's Main Street after school on Mondays, Tuesdays, and Thursdays, and all day Saturday, Extraordinary Ernie and Marvelous Maud were such great friends that sometimes Ernie almost forgot she was a sheep.

Drawing closer, Ernie noticed that Maud looked different. As well as her usual short pink cape, she was wearing an enormous floppy velvet hat.

"Hi, Maud," he said, on reaching her. "Nice hat."

"Thanks, Ernie," said Maud. "It's called a beret. Artists wear them."

Ernie nodded his understanding. Maud had recently begun taking art classes. "How are your classes going?" he asked, as they started to stroll along Main Street toward the town hall, on the lookout for wrongdoers and mischief-makers.

"Oh, they're great, Ernie!" said Maud enthusiastically. "Today I started work on a self-porpoise."

"A self-por—?"

"A self-porpoise," said Maud. "It's when you paint a picture of yourself. Maybe when I'm done I could do a porpoise of you, hey, partner?"

"Er, yeah," said Ernie. "That would be great."

"Anyway," said Maud, "how was your day? Busy? I thought you were going to be late."

"I had to stop at the library on my way home from school," Ernie explained. "I'm doing research for a school project. We have to write about our heroes."

"Oh wow, that sounds really interesting," said Maud. "Are you going to write about The Daring Dynamo?" The Daring Dynamo was a TV superhero, and Ernie never missed an episode of his show.

"No," said Ernie sadly. "My teacher told me I'm not allowed to do any more projects on The Daring Dynamo."

"Oh, that's tough," said Maud sympathetically.

"So who will your project be on then?"

"That's the problem," said Ernie. "I don't know. But I've borrowed a book from the library called *The Greatest Heroes in History*, so there's bound to be someone in that."

"*The Greatest Heroes in History* . . ." said Maud. "That sounds fascinating. Are there many sheep in the book?"

"Um, I don't think so," said Ernie doubtfully.

"Oh, I see, the sheep are in a separate book, are they? Maybe one called *The Greatest Sheep Heroes in History*?"

"I didn't see a book like that," said Ernie.

"Oh," said Maud. She looked dismayed. "Isn't there anything at all about heroic sheep in the library?"

Fortunately, Ernie was saved from answering when Maud suddenly trotted briskly up the pavement to throw her woolly bulk in front of a toddler who was about to run onto the road. The child's grateful parents thanked her profusely, and by the time Ernie caught up, Maud was smiling again.

"Do you know what, Ernie?" she said, as they crossed the road and began to walk down the other side of Main Street toward the park at the end of the block. "I'll bet we see lots of heroes at the conference!"

Ernie and Maud wouldn't be patrolling Main

Street as usual this Saturday. Along with the four original members of the Superheroes Society (Baxter Branch)—Super Whiz, Valiant Vera, Amazing Desmond, and Housecat Woman— they were going to spend the weekend at the National Superheroes Conference in Thomastown.

Ernie could hardly wait. He and Maud would get to see hundreds of superheroes, and even meet other trainee superheroes and sidekicks. Plus there were all kinds of interesting courses and classes. But, best of all, Super Whiz, the president of the Superheroes Society (Baxter Branch), had been invited to give a speech.

Of course, Ernie and Maud had heard Super Whiz give speeches many times before, as he held regular Monday afternoon training sessions for the two new recruits. Ernie had to admit that some of Super Whiz's speeches were just a little bit dull. But he was so proud to think that their very own president would be speaking in front of all the other superheroes in the country that he would have gladly listened to a hundred speeches on "Ideal Cape Length: Below the Knee or above

the Knee?" or "Perfect Patrol Pacing: Brisk Walk or Energetic Amble?"

It was a slow afternoon on patrol—though Ernie twice had to rescue Maud when her beret slipped over her eyes and she walked into a bush—and the two trainees spent the rest of the afternoon talking excitedly about the conference. When they got back to 32 Main Street to report in at the end of their patrol, they found that the superheroes were also talking about the conference.

"Maps," Super Whiz was saying importantly as Ernie and Maud pushed open the shabby brown door. He, Valiant Vera, and Amazing Desmond were sitting around the long table in the middle of the room. Housecat Woman was asleep in her usual armchair. "Since I am the brains of the Baxter Branch, I suppose it will be up to me to navigate all the way to Thomastown. And if I am to do that successfully, I will need *very* detailed maps."

"And snacks," broke in Amazing Desmond, tipping Ernie and Maud a cheery wink. "If I am to drive all the way to Thomastown successfully, I will need *very* detailed snacks."

Super Whiz sighed in frustration. "Can't you ever be serious, Desmond?"

"Sorry, Whiz!" said Amazing Desmond, who, as far as Ernie knew, had never been serious. Then, noticing Super Whiz's furious glare, Desmond corrected himself. "I mean Super." Super Whiz hated to be called Whiz.

"Hello, you two," said Valiant Vera, waving at Ernie and Maud. "Are you looking forward to the conference?" Valiant Vera was not only incredibly brave and strong, she was also one of the kindest people Ernie had ever met.

"We sure are!" said Maud happily.

The two trainees gave their patrol report then bid the superheroes goodbye.

"Remember," Super Whiz called after them, "we leave at nine o'clock sharp on Saturday."

"And bring snacks!" chimed in Desmond.

"Oh, and Maud? Superhero costume only," Valiant Vera said with a meaningful look at Maud's beret.

"Yes, Vera," said Maud meekly.

It wasn't until they were back outside on Main Street, about to go their separate ways, that Maud raised the subject of heroic sheep again. "Ernie," she said, "can you think of any great heroic sheep in history? Even one?"

"No," Ernie had to admit. "But I'm sure there are some," he added, seeing the disappointment on Maud's face.

As he watched Maud clip-clop slowly down Main Street toward the park, Ernie was determined that he would find them.

TWO

Ernie woke bright and early on Saturday morning and immediately pulled on his fluorescent green one-piece suit with the gold lightning bolts on the sleeves, and fastened his matching cape around his neck. He had breakfast in front of the television, but switched it off even before seeing if The Daring Dynamo managed to escape the clutches of the dastardly Count Crustaceous. This was one morning when Ernie definitely did not want to be late. He brushed his teeth, said goodbye to his parents, then picked up his school backpack, into which he'd packed his pajamas and the library's copy of *The Greatest Heroes in History*.

As he jogged down the street, Ernie felt a bit anxious about the fact that he hadn't yet found a single sheep hero in the book, even though he'd read two chapters already: "Excellent Explorers" and "Super Sports Stars."

But when he arrived at the Superheroes Society (Baxter Branch) headquarters at ten to nine, Ernie saw that he needn't have worried. Maud, who was already there, was her usual good-humored self.

"Hi partner," she called happily, when she spotted Ernie. "Look at this—a van! I've never been in a van before!"

Sure enough, a white van was parked at the curb. Standing beside it, each holding a small suitcase, were Super Whiz, Valiant Vera, and Housecat Woman. Ernie thought he'd never seen their costumes look so shiny and neatly pressed.

Super Whiz was looking at his watch and muttering impatiently. "What's taking him so long? I've told him a thousand times how important it is that we are punctual."

"Don't worry," Valiant Vera said soothingly. "I'm sure he'll be out in a minute."

She had barely finished her sentence when Amazing Desmond came bustling through the shabby brown door with two enormous suitcases.

"Goodness me," said Vera. "What on earth have you packed, Desmond? We're only going for one night."

"Just a few essentials," Desmond assured her. "Tuxedo, in case of a ball. Snorkel and flippers, in case there's a coral reef in Thomastown. Chaps, in case we go horse riding . . ."

Super Whiz was turning purple. "This is a serious conference, Desmond, about important matters. We are there to learn from our colleagues, to study new—"

"Keep your shirt on, Whiz," Desmond said mildly.

Valiant Vera gave Desmond a sharp nudge in the ribs with her elbow and whispered something that Ernie didn't quite catch, though he thought he heard the words "nervous" and "speech."

Desmond nodded at what Vera was saying, then turned to the others and said, "Well, what are you standing around for? Let's go!"

They all bustled forward to stow their suitcases, then Desmond slid open the side door of the van to reveal two rows of seats, three at the back and two at the front.

Housecat Woman, who could move surprisingly quickly when she was awake, was first in. She made straight for the back row, stretched out along the three seats, and promptly fell asleep.

"Ernie, you and Maud take the two seats there," Valiant Vera instructed. "I'll sit up front between Super and Desmond." To keep the peace, Ernie suspected.

"Ooh, Ernie, can I have the window seat? Please, please, please?" Maud was hopping excitedly from hoof to hoof.

"Of course you can, Maud," said Ernie generously. He'd ridden in a van many times.

After a bit of a struggle with Maud's seatbelt — "You'd almost think these were designed with no idea of the shape of a sheep," Maud complained — they were on their way.

"Jingle bells, jingle bells," sang Amazing Desmond as he drove down Main Street.

"Could you please stop that infernal racket," grumbled Super Whiz. "How am I meant to concentrate on my maps with you caterwauling like that — oops!" He clapped a hand over his mouth and glanced at the back seat to see if Housecat Woman had taken offense, but she was snoring away in a dreamy doze.

"Sorry, Whiz," said Desmond. He took one hand off the steering wheel and mimed buttoning up his lips.

"And keep both hands on the steering wheel!" Super Whiz yelped.

"Sorry, Whiz," said Desmond again, though he didn't really sound sorry.

"And don't call me Whiz," snapped Super Whiz.

"Oops. Sorry, Whiz," said Desmond.

"I *said*—"

"Could you show me Thomastown on the map?" Vera asked Super Whiz. "I have no idea where it is."

"Of course," said Super Whiz, who liked it when people recognized his superior knowledge. "Now, we're going to follow this road for another fifty miles, then you see this highway here . . ."

"Oh, show me, show me," begged Maud. "I've never seen a map before. Sheep don't use maps."

"But how do you find your way?" asked Super Whiz, puzzled.

"You just follow the sheep in front of you," Maud said.

An hour later, they were on the highway. Ernie was reading chapter three of *The Greatest Heroes in History*, all about "Marvels of Medicine" (still

no mention of sheep), and Maud had her nose out the window. Ernie could just hear a faint "Wheeee!" as Housecat Woman snored softly behind them. Amazing Desmond and Super Whiz were still arguing.

"Please observe the speed limit, Desmond," Super Whiz was saying stiffly.

"Sorry, Whiz," said Desmond.

"And don't call me Whiz," said Super Whiz through clenched teeth.

"Oops. I can't believe I did it again! Sorry, Whiz," said Desmond.

"I *said*—"

"Why don't I read you the conference program?" broke in Valiant Vera, holding up a brochure. Ernie thought the back of her head looked weary.

"Let's see . . . Well, we'll have a little while to settle in, then there's going to be a welcome address before dinner. After that we should aim to have an early night as we have a busy day tomorrow. Oh look—the closing address tomorrow afternoon will be given by The Daring Dynamo. How nice."

Ernie sat bolt upright. "The Daring Dynamo?" he gasped. "He's—he's my hero!"

"That's right," agreed Maud, whose fleece was looking a little windswept. "Ernie talks about him all the time."

"Dynamo?" said Desmond. "He's a good sort."

"I suppose he's all right," conceded Super Whiz.

"All right?" squawked Ernie. "He's the bravest, fastest, daringest, most heroic—Well, who's your hero, Super Whiz?"

Super Whiz sniffed. "No one. Superheroes are heroes, they don't have heroes."

"Oh, now, that's not true, Super Whiz," Vera objected. "Superheroes have heroes too."

"Who's your hero, Valiant Vera?" Ernie asked curiously.

"Hmm . . . Marie Curie," said Vera, after giving it some thought.

"Is she brave and strong and fast like you?" Ernie said.

"Oh no!" Vera laughed. "She was a famous scientist."

"What about you, Amazing Desmond?" Ernie wanted to know. "Do you have a hero?"

"Ronald," said Desmond promptly.

Super Whiz snorted.

"Desmond," Vera chided, "the pizza delivery man is not heroic."

"But he can make a Super-Triple-Supremo Supreme with extra cheese and pepperoni and deliver it to your door piping hot in thirteen and a half minutes!" Desmond protested. "Speaking of which . . ."

With a screech of tires he steered the van off the highway and into the parking lot of a roadside restaurant. "Lunchtime!" he announced.

They all got out of the van and stretched, and Maud trotted briskly around the parking lot a couple of times to make sure her hooves still worked. "Sheep aren't really used to sitting down," she confided to Ernie as they filed into the restaurant.

The four superheroes and two trainees crowded into a booth and examined the menus.

"Ah, yes," said Desmond when a waiter approached to take their order. "I'll have a nice big juicy steak . . . I mean—" Desmond broke off and looked uncertainly at Maud, whose face was still buried in the menu. Maud was a strict vegetarian.

"Salad," Ernie supplied helpfully. "I'll have a salad, please."

"Me too," said Super Whiz quickly.

"Er, me three," said Desmond, a bit sadly.

"And me," said Valiant Vera.

"A small bowl of milk, please," said Housecat Woman.

Maud looked up at the sea of expectant faces. "My turn? Well, you all mightn't be hungry," she said, "but I'm starving. I'll have the macaroni and cheese with extra cheese, a big piece of apple pie with cream and ice cream, and a chocolate milkshake, please."

A few minutes later Super Whiz looked anxiously at his watch. "I do hope they'll be quick. We don't want to be late."

"Why, Whiz? Are you afraid we'll get in trouble?" teased Desmond.

"Don't be ridiculous," said Super Whiz indignantly. "Superheroes aren't afraid of anything!"

Desmond guffawed. "Oh, come on, Whiz!" he said. "Of course they are. Superheroes are only human—"

"Not sheep," Ernie heard Maud mutter to herself.

"—we have fears too."

"What are you afraid of, Amazing Desmond?" asked Ernie, as the waiter returned with their lunch.

"Cold, soggy pizza," said Desmond, poking miserably at a lettuce leaf and casting a longing look at Maud's extra-cheesy macaroni.

"I'm afraid of dogs," Maud said. "Big black dogs with sharp teeth."

"Me too," said Housecat Woman between sips of milk.

"What about you, Valiant Vera?" Maud asked. "What's your greatest fear?"

"I don't know," said Valiant Vera thoughtfully. "Lots of things, I expect." But after giving the matter some consideration, she shook her head.

It appeared she couldn't think of any.

Ernie was secretly pleased when Super Whiz tapped his watch and said, "Eat quickly, everyone." If he'd had to list all his fears—bullies, big waves, getting locked in a trunk, sharks, stampeding elephants—they would have still been there at dinnertime! The more he learned about heroes, the less sure he was that he would ever really be one.

THREE

It was almost three o'clock by the time the super-heroes of Baxter Branch arrived in Thomastown.

"Very nice," Vera said approvingly as they passed under a banner that read: *Thomastown welcomes superheroes to the National Superheroes Conference.*

"Follow the signs to the Pleasant Dayz Conference Center," Super Whiz instructed.

They drove down a main street that was every bit as busy and bustling as Baxter was on a Saturday afternoon, then crossed a river over a small stone bridge and turned into a driveway next to a sign reading, *Enjoy your stayz at Pleasant Dayz.*

When they pulled into the parking lot, Ernie saw dozens of vans just like theirs—and dozens of superheroes.

"Look, Maud," he whispered. Milling around with suitcases and backpacks and baskets and boxes were superheroes of all shapes and sizes: tall and thin, and short and plump; tall and plump, and short and thin. And although Ernie couldn't see any other sheep, he did see a small scattering of animal sidekicks.

The air was filled with a happy buzz.

"What a lovely pair of tights!"

"Thank you, they're new."

"I hope the dinner menu is better than last time."

". . . big and red, but he won't be flying in until tomorrow."

"Ah, Dynamo always arrives in style . . ."

"Look, it's Magnificent Marjory from Beezerville Branch! Marjory, over here!" called Valiant Vera, waving at a muscular woman dressed in yellow.

Magnificent Marjory gave a whoop and

swooped over like a giant canary.

"Vera!" she said, giving the other woman a hug. "Ah, Super Whiz, I'm looking forward to your speech tomorrow. Desmond, handsome as ever, I see." Desmond turned red and tried to suck in his tummy, which was poking through the gap between his orange top and purple tights. "And Housecat Woman—keeping the mice at bay, I hope?"

"These are our trainees, Extraordinary Ernie and Marvelous Maud," Vera said, gesturing at them.

"I'm very pleased to meet you," said Magnificent Marjory. "Vera has told me a lot about you. Beezerville Branch has brought a couple of trainees along too. You should keep an eye out for them; I'm sure you'd have plenty to talk about. Well, must dash—registration is through there." She pointed toward a table on a patch of grass at the edge of the parking lot. "See you later!"

The superheroes holding their suitcases, Maud carrying a straw basket between her teeth, and Ernie with his backpack slung over his shoulder headed for the line snaking back from the registration table.

"Right," said Vera, when they had signed in. "We've got two cabins, 37B and 37C."

"A cabin?" Maud, who had put down her basket, gave a happy skip. "I've never slept in a cabin before! Though I did sleep in a barn once, when I was a little lamb . . ."

Following a map they had been given at the registration table, they found their small wooden cabins at the edge of a field opposite the cafeteria and a large assembly hall.

"This will do very nicely," said Vera with a nod, as she opened the door to the first cabin to reveal a bunk bed against one wall and a single

bed against the other.

Housecat Woman, who was good at climbing and liked high places, quickly claimed the top bunk, and Maud, who liked neither, put her basket down on the bottom.

Super Whiz led Ernie and Desmond to the cabin next door, which had an identical layout. Super Whiz quickly claimed the single bed.

"You'd best take the top bunk, Ernie," Desmond decided. "I'm not as nimble with ladders as I used to be."

There was a crackle, then an officious voice boomed over a loudspeaker: "The welcoming address will begin in fifteen minutes. Please make your way to the assembly hall. I repeat: the welcoming address will begin in fifteen minutes."

The members of Baxter Branch emerged from their cabins and joined the throng of superheroes hurrying toward the assembly hall.

"This is amazing," Ernie whispered to Maud when they were at last seated in a middle row of the large hall. "I've never seen so many superheroes!"

Their attention was drawn to the stage as a small round woman with glasses and curly hair tapped the microphone and said, "Ahem," in a high voice. Her one-piece orange costume and cape shimmered with silver stars.

"That's Stupendous Sue," whispered Amazing Desmond, who was seated on the other side of Ernie. "She's the president of the Superheroes Society National Headquarters—she's stupendously well organized and very, very smart.

In fact," he continued, lowering his voice even further, "*she's* Whiz's hero."

Clearly he hadn't lowered his voice low enough, because Super Whiz, who was sitting on the other side of Maud, hissed, "Shhh. Don't be ridiculous." But Ernie noticed he was blushing.

"I would like to welcome you all to this year's National Superheroes Conference," the president was saying. "For my welcoming address today, I've chosen the topic 'Superheroing for a Safer Society.'"

Wow! Ernie couldn't imagine a more interesting or important topic. It seemed that the other superheroes were equally interested, as all the murmuring and whispering died down and the audience sat up a little straighter.

"In the age of the internet," Stupendous Sue began, reading from a sheaf of papers. But before the eager audience could learn how the internet related to Superheroing for a Safer Society, there was a blur of red and white as someone streaked across the stage—and snatched Stupendous Sue's notes straight out of her hands!

"Stop, thief!" cried Stupendous Sue.

Two hundred superheroes stared at each other then back at the stage, aghast. Who would dare steal from the president of the Superheroes Society—in front of a hall full of superheroes?!

Then there was a strange cackle and a thin voice rang out across the room:

Run, run, as fast as you can,
You can't catch me—
I'm Chicken George!

FOUR

On stage, the president was looking more stupe-fied than stupendous.

"Quick, everyone," she urged. "After him!"

As one, the assembled superheroes rose and surged toward the door.

To Ernie's surprise, there was a lot of pushing and shoving. He'd always imagined that super-heroes would be super polite, but apparently this wasn't the case.

"You might be Fast Freddie," a young black-clad woman said to a man in pink and aqua stripes, "but I'm Hasty Harriet, so step aside."

"Oh yeah?" said a wiry older woman, pushing past them. "Well, the pair of you can make way for Rapid Rebecca!"

Ernie was surrounded on all sides by similar complaints.

"Watch it, you're standing on my cape!"

"Get your big fat feet off my toes of steel!"

And, most disturbing of all, "What's that sheep doing here? This conference is reserved for heroes, not barnyard animals!"

Ernie spun around angrily to see a pear-shaped man in a tight white costume. There was a sudden streak of black and claws, then the man stared disbelievingly at his tattered sleeve.

"My sleeve—you've torn it to shreds!" he shrieked.

"Sorry," purred Housecat Woman sweetly. Ernie glanced anxiously at Maud, hoping she hadn't heard the exchange, but he could tell by her downcast eyes that she had.

At last the crowd of superheroes gushed from the assembly hall like water from a tap onto the field outside.

Fast Freddie, Hasty Harriet, and Rapid Rebecca raced around the field, and Eagle-eyed Ed and his twin brother, Beady-eyed Bert, scanned the grass for clues. But there was not a thieving chicken in sight.

"Who is Chicken George?" Ernie asked Amazing Desmond, who was standing beside him.

Desmond shrugged. "Search me," he said. "This is the first I've heard of him." He turned to Magnificent Marjory, who had just walked up. "Have you heard of this Chicken George before, Marj?"

"Not a word," said Marjory.

"He's probably part of some evil new barn-yard gang," chimed in the pear-shaped man, who clearly didn't like sheep.

"Which specializes in stealing speeches?" asked Rapid Rebecca, still panting from her circuit of the field.

Seeing there was nothing more they could do, the gathering moved toward the cafeteria for dinner.

After helping themselves at the buffet— "There's some great vegetarian dishes," Maud noted excitedly, with Desmond adding, "And pepperoni pizza!"—they found seats at one of the four long tables.

All conversation centered around the outrageous nerve of Chicken George. While Ernie had seen little more than a flash of white with a crest of red whiz across the stage, it appeared that many others in the audience had had a closer look.

"Seven feet tall!" said one.

"With a beak as sharp as a knife!" said another.

"And giant fangs!" added a third.

The one thing everyone agreed on was that Chicken George was the most terrifying and villainous chicken anyone had ever seen.

Ernie shivered. Suddenly he had a new fear to add to his long list.

"The question is," said Super Whiz loudly, thumping his fist on the table, "what are we going to do about it? We can't just have criminal chickens waltzing in and stealing speeches from our president."

"Well, he didn't exactly waltz," Desmond pointed out. "He moved across that stage faster than a speeding pizza driver. I've never seen a chicken move so fast!"

Stupendous Sue, who was sitting a few places away at the head of the table, said firmly, "Super Whiz is right. No one is safe while that chicken is on the loose. I'm going to hold a meeting of all branch presidents tomorrow morning so we can develop a plan of action."

With that decided, the assembled super-heroes seemed to feel that they could turn their attention to dinner. Ernie was impressed by their heroic appetites.

When all the plates and bowls were finally scraped clean, and even Desmond had eaten his fill from the dessert buffet, superheroes began to rise from their seats and drift off toward their cabins.

Valiant Vera was studying the conference schedule as the members of Baxter Branch crossed the darkening field. "I've signed you two up for a seminar that starts straight after breakfast," she told Ernie and Maud. "'Terrific Trainees and Super Sidekicks: Creating Tomorrow's Superheroes Today.'"

Ernie and Maud exchanged delighted looks. "That sounds great!" Maud said.

"Super Whiz will be at the meeting of branch presidents, of course," Valiant Vera continued.

"Of course," Super Whiz echoed importantly.

"Desmond, you're down for—" Vera squinted at her schedule. "'Card Games and Line Dancing' . . . ?"

"Er, that should read '"Hard Names and Line Glancing,'" said Desmond quickly. "It's, um, a class on how to use the telephone book to hunt down mischief-makers."

"Oh!" said Vera, looking surprised. "Okay. Housecat Woman will be going to a class on 'Superhero Stress Relief: From Rescuing to Relaxing,' and I am attending a seminar on 'Equipment and Resource Management,' which I expect will be very valuable. We'll all meet up again at Super Whiz's lecture in the main assembly hall, then have some lunch before The Daring Dynamo gives the closing address."

As they filed into their cabins, Ernie noticed that Maud was lagging behind.

"What are you doing, Maud?" His sidekick was standing still, gazing up at the sky. Bathed in moonlight, her fleece looked snowy white.

"I'm just looking at the moon, Ernie," Maud said with a sigh. "I was thinking about the first astronauts, and wondering if a sheep

will ever do something so heroic."

"Oh Maud, I'm sure there have been plenty of heroic sheep," said Ernie. "Um, what about . . . I know! What about that black sheep? You know, the one who had all that wool. Three whole bags, wasn't it?"

"You mean Blackie? Oh, she's all right, I suppose, but I'd hardly count being able to grow a lot of wool as heroic, Ernie."

"Hmm, I suppose you're right," Ernie had to admit. "Wait!" he said desperately as Maud turned and slowly made her way toward her cabin.

"What about those sheep you count when you're trying to get to sleep? They have saved millions of people from sleepless nights!"

"Thanks for trying, Ernie," Maud said. "But we both know those sheep are imaginary. Let's face it: sheep can't be heroes."

"Well, I'll tell you something, Maud," Ernie called after her. "If a chicken can be a villain, then a sheep can definitely be a hero."

"Thanks for trying, Ernie," Maud said again. "Goodnight."

"Goodnight, Maud." Ernie trudged into his cabin. Even though the lights were still on, Desmond was already snoring away. Super Whiz was sitting up in bed reading through his speech and muttering to himself.

Ernie changed into his pajamas, brushed his teeth, then climbed up to his bunk with *The Greatest Heroes in History*. He might as well read another chapter before going to sleep—perhaps there would be a sheep in this chapter.

"Fearless Heroes of Flight," he read, his eyes starting to feel heavy already.

By the time Super Whiz turned out the light, Ernie was fast asleep and dreaming that he was counting sheep jumping over a fence. Each sheep wore a short pink cape that fluttered as it jumped, and each one turned to him and said sadly, "Sheep can't be heroes."

FIVE

When Ernie stepped outside the next morning, he scanned the grounds anxiously for any sign of a seven-foot chicken with enormous teeth. Instead, he saw a huge, red hot-air balloon tethered at the far end of the field.

"A hot-air balloon!" he said to Amazing Desmond, who was right behind him. "Where did it come from?"

"Ah, The Daring Dynamo must have arrived," Desmond said. He peered at a small shape moving around the balloon's basket. "Yep, that looks like Clever Clementine."

Ernie peered too, and could just make out a small white body with vivid orange legs and a bright orange beak. "A duck?" he guessed.

"That's right. Clementine is Dynamo's sidekick, and a great one."

The Daring Dynamo had an animal sidekick, just like he did! They had never mentioned that on TV. Ernie couldn't wait to tell Maud. He spotted her a little way ahead, staring at the balloon as if transfixed.

"Look, Ernie," she breathed, as he came to stand beside her. "Have you ever seen anything more beautiful? Wouldn't you love to have a ride?"

"Yeah!" said Ernie. Then he said honestly, and a little glumly, "Well, no, not really. I'd be too scared to go so high."

Maud looked shocked. "Scared, Ernie? You? But you're so brave! Remember how you climbed that tall tree to rescue my sister Mavis?"

"That was different," Ernie tried to explain. "Mavis was in danger. I didn't stop to think."

"Well, I'd love to ride in a hot-air balloon,"

Maud said dreamily. Then her face fell. "But it's probably one more thing that sheep can't do."

Picturing Maud in a hot-air balloon, Ernie had a sudden flash of memory. "Maud!" he said excitedly. "Sheep *can* fly in hot-air balloons! Not only that, the first-ever pilot of a hot-air balloon was a sheep!" Maud listened, enthralled, as Ernie repeated what he'd read in "Fearless Heroes of Flight" the night before. "The first hot-air balloon was launched in 1783, and the pilots were a sheep, a duck, and a rooster," he told her. "And they stayed aloft for fifteen whole minutes."

"Oh Ernie!" Maud exclaimed. "Is this true?"

"It's all in the book, Maud," Ernie assured her. "A sheep was one of the greatest heroes of flight." It was a proud Maud who cantered across the field to breakfast.

When Ernie and Maud joined Amazing Desmond, Valiant Vera, and Housecat Woman in the front row of the assembly hall for Super Whiz's speech, they were both feeling much more heroic than they had the previous day.

"How did you enjoy your seminar?" Valiant Vera asked them.

"It was great!" the two trainees chorused.

Their instructor, a jovial woman who had reminded them a bit of Desmond, had been very encouraging. They'd role-played several super-heroic scenarios, and Lion-hearted Lakmi had held up Ernie and Maud as an example of a part-nership that worked exceptionally well.

"Well done, you two," said Valiant Vera, sounding pleased. "And what about the other trainee superheroes and sidekicks — were they nice? Did you meet the pair from Beezerville?"

"Er, yes," said Ernie. He and Maud looked at each other and tried not to laugh. "Very nice." Trainee superhero Mei-Li had indeed been very nice, but her sidekick, Cuddles, was a very pompous porcupine.

"Is The Daring Dynamo here?" Ernie asked,

craning his head around.

Vera laughed. "Oh no. Dynamo will be hiding out until it's time to give his speech. He's quite shy, really."

"Shhh." Amazing Desmond flapped his hands at them. "Super Whiz is about to begin." Looking up at the stage, Ernie saw Super Whiz standing at the microphone. His blue tights looked very stylish, and the red SW stamped on his chest seemed to positively glow under the lights. But to Ernie's surprise, Super Whiz, who loved giving speeches, was pale and trembling.

"Is Super Whiz worried that Chicken George might steal his speech?" he asked Desmond.

Desmond shook his head. "I think Whiz would be glad if Chicken George turned up now," he said. "It's not Chicken George that he's afraid of—he's nervous about speaking in front of such a big audience."

Just then, Super Whiz glanced down at them anxiously. And although Ernie had only ever seen them arguing, Amazing Desmond gave Super Whiz an encouraging thumbs-up.

With a grateful smile, Super Whiz began . . .

Desmond had bet Ernie a double-scoop colossal chocolate ice cream cone that Super Whiz's speech would be all about Leadership, since that was his favorite subject, but instead the Baxter Branch president had chosen Teamwork as his theme. Ernie was embarrassed but pleased to find that he and Maud were mentioned several times.

When Super Whiz finished talking there was a huge wave of applause and people rushed forward to congratulate him. Some wanted to talk to Ernie and Maud and the other members of Baxter Branch too, and they were surrounded by people as they exited the hall and walked toward the cafeteria for lunch. Mei-Li waved a friendly greeting as they passed her, and even Cuddles looked impressed.

Lunchtime chatter was all about the heroes of Baxter Branch and their town's record low levels of wrongdoing. Ernie even heard one superhero say to another, "I bet Chicken George wouldn't have gotten away with that speech-stealing stunt in Baxter." After a while, though, he started to find all the attention overwhelming. As soon as he had an opportunity he slipped outside for a bit of peace and quiet and to look for Maud, who had left the hall a little earlier.

At first he saw no sign of his partner, but a glance toward the far end of the field told him exactly where she was: sitting in the basket of the hot-air balloon. Walking closer, he could see that Clever Clementine was waving 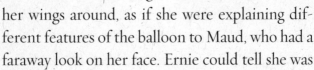 her wings around, as if she were explaining different features of the balloon to Maud, who had a faraway look on her face. Ernie could tell she was thinking of that heroic sheep who had piloted one of the first-ever flights.

As Ernie made his way across the grass toward the balloon, he was suddenly overtaken by a streak of red and white.

Oh no! Chicken George!

"Maud!" Ernie cried. "Watch out!"

Maud looked up just in time to see Chicken George, who had nimbly untied the rope tethering the balloon to the ground, dive into the basket.

There came a mad cackle, and then, just like the night before, a thin voice rang out in a strange song:

Run, run, as fast as you can,
You can't catch me—
I'm Chicken George!

"MAUD!" Ernie yelled, racing toward the balloon, which was slowly lifting from the ground.

But the basket was already hovering just beyond his reach. With a desperate lunge, Ernie grabbed the rope that was trailing like a tail behind the balloon, which was picking up speed as a gust of wind blew it higher.

"Ernie!"

Looking up, Ernie could see the anxious faces of a duck and sheep gazing down at him.

"Let go, Ernie!" Maud urged. "Save yourself while there's still time."

Ernie shook his head. He was petrified but determined. As long as Maud was trapped in that basket with a vicious, villainous chicken, he was hanging on.

Glancing down, Ernie saw a sea of curious faces as the superheroes spilled out onto the field after lunch.

"Hey!" someone cried. "Up in the air! It's The Daring Dynamo's balloon."

"But Dynamo's backstage working on his speech," said someone else. "So who's piloting that thing?"

There was a pause, and then the first voice said in a tone of disbelief, "A sheep, a duck, and — is that a rooster?"

"No," called Ernie

breathlessly, clutching the rope as he was lifted higher and higher above their heads. "It's Chicken George!"

SIX

The balloon was soon sailing high above Thomastown, with Ernie dangling below. From this angle, Thomastown didn't look nearly as welcoming as it had the day before.

He could hear nothing over the rushing wind in his ears as they swept above the town's main street. He shivered at the thought of poor Maud and Clementine, cornered in the basket by the monstrous chicken.

The problem was, Ernie realized, as the town below grew smaller and smaller, he wasn't much use to Maud and Clementine where he was.

"Maud," he called faintly. "Are you okay?" But his words were blown away by the breeze.

Tentatively, Ernie took one hand from the rope and moved it higher, then did the same with the other hand. He continued climbing slowly, hand over hand, trying not to think of what might happen if a strong gust of wind hit him while he had only one hand on the rope. Soon he was closer to the basket, but the muscles in his arms were so sore and tired they were trembling. He knew he couldn't hold on much longer.

"Maud!" he cried. "Maud, can you hear me?"

There was a pause, long enough to make Ernie's pulse race in terror for his friend, then Maud's voice said reassuringly, "We're fine, Ernie. You hold on tight and Clementine will have us down in a jiffy."

Ernie was comforted, if puzzled. What had happened to Chicken George?

To his relief, the balloon appeared to have altered course and was now heading back across the river toward the Pleasant Dayz Conference Center.

He closed his eyes for a moment, weak with exhaustion, and when he opened them again he was level with the treetops surrounding the field.

As they descended gently toward the open ground, two hundred concerned superheroes were visible once more, and this time Ernie could make out the superheroes of Baxter Branch. They had pushed to the front of the crowd and, as Ernie's feet touched the ground, they came running toward him.

Ernie watched anxiously as the balloon's basket hit the earth with a gentle thump. Clementine was moving efficiently around the basket, pulling ropes, while Maud appeared to be in deep conversation with—not a chicken, but a thin, shamefaced young man with bright red hair.

The young man leapt from the basket, then turned to give Maud a helping hand. Valiant Vera, who was the fastest of the Baxter superheroes, arrived at Ernie's side just as Maud did, with Housecat Woman, Super Whiz, and Amazing Desmond close behind.

Vera threw her arms around Ernie as

Desmond threw his arms around Maud, then Vera gave Maud a big squeeze as Desmond gave Ernie a hearty hug. Super Whiz patted them both vigorously, and Housecat Woman curled around all of them affectionately.

"*That's* what I'm afraid of," panted Vera, when she had gotten her breath back. She was speaking as if they were still at the roadside restaurant talking about their fears. "I'm afraid of bad things happening to the people I care about."

Ernie thought it was one of the most noble fears he'd ever heard.

Just then he noticed that the expressions of relief coming from the crowd of watching superheroes had turned into dark muttering. Then someone said loudly, "He's not so tall."

And someone said even louder, "His teeth don't look so big."

And a third person called, "He's not even a chicken!"

The crowd surged forward and Ernie could hear furious cries of, "Where's Stupendous Sue's speech?" and "What's the big idea of stealing The Daring Dynamo's balloon?" and "Why do you call yourself a chicken?!"

The red-haired man standing near the Baxter Branch superheroes began to look frightened as the angry crowd drew nearer.

Suddenly, Maud leapt in front of Chicken George and held up a hoof.

"Wait!" she shouted.

Still muttering, the assembled superheroes stopped.

"This is George," said Maud, waving her hoof at the frightened young man. "And he lives here in Thomastown. All his life, people have mocked him because of his sticking-up red hair. Because it looked like a chicken's crest, they called him Chicken George—and they said he must *be* a chicken."

"Oh, that's harsh," said one red-haired super-hero standing near the front of the crowd. There were a few murmurs of sympathy.

"Finally," Maud continued, "all the teasing and taunting became too much and George decided to act. When he heard that the National Superheroes Conference was being held here, he thought he'd show everyone that he wasn't a chicken by outsmarting the fastest and fleetest and bravest and cleverest people in the country: the superheroes."

A few of the superheroes snorted indignantly, but others were nodding their heads.

"It's true," said one. "We are fast and fleet."

"Though not as fast and fleet as Chicken George," another pointed out.

"Come here, George," said Maud, beckoning. Chicken George shuffled forward to stand beside her. "Now George knows he has behaved badly, don't you, George?" Maud nudged the young man.

Chicken George nodded.

"And he has something he would like to say."

Chicken George cleared his throat, and when he spoke Ernie was surprised to hear that his voice was quite ordinary, without a hint of a cackle.

"I'm very sorry," Chicken George mumbled. He looked over at Maud, who nodded encouragingly. "I did a stupid thing. I know now how foolish I was—Marvelous Maud has helped me to see that I was hurting the very people who would have helped me. I'm sorry," he said again.

Stupendous Sue stepped forward. "Well, I accept your apology, George," she said, and the crowd murmured their agreement. "Now," she announced, "it's time we all made our way to the hall to hear The Daring Dynamo's speech. Thank you, Marvelous Maud," she added, turning to address the sheep. "You've done well. Very well indeed."

Ernie thought he would burst with pride as Maud trotted over to join him and the members of the Superheroes Society (Baxter Branch).

Strolling slowly across the field toward the assembly hall with the others, Ernie caught a

glimpse of a duck talking animatedly to a tall, dashing man dressed all in red standing at the edge of the field. The duck was gesturing with her wings to George, and once her left wing seemed to point at Maud, then at Ernie.

The dark-haired man nodded thoughtfully, then glanced in the direction the duck was pointing.

When Ernie caught a look at the man's face, his heart almost stopped. It was The Daring Dynamo!

SEVEN

It felt strange to Ernie to be sitting back in the same seat in the front row of the assembly hall after everything that had happened since Super Whiz's speech. It felt especially strange to be so close to his hero, The Daring Dynamo. He had always seemed like a distant figure who only existed on TV—but no, he was real, and he was so close Ernie could almost reach out and touch him.

"Good afternoon, fellow superheroes," The Daring Dynamo began. "And what an action-packed afternoon it has been."

Many members of the audience murmured

their agreement.

"On witnessing the happy resolution of what looked like a certain tragedy, I have started to question the nature of heroism. What, my dear colleagues, is a hero? Is it the bravest, strongest and fastest among us?"

As The Daring Dynamo stood up straight, his muscles bulging, Ernie began to nod, as did many others.

"Or is a hero the most intelligent and wise among us?"

Ernie saw Super Whiz nodding.

"I think not," said The Daring Dynamo simply, provoking gasps from the audience. "Let us consider the actions of Marvelous Maud of Baxter Branch," he continued, gesturing to the front row, where Maud sat dumbstruck. "Did not this heroic sheep transform a vicious, terrifying chicken monster into an ordinary young man?"

The superheroes in the audience had to admit it was so.

The Daring Dynamo was right, Ernie realized. The Chicken George who had stolen

Stupendous Sue's speech and The Daring Dynamo's hot-air balloon was a far different character from the young man who now sat between Maud and Clementine in the front row.

"And how did she do that?" The Daring Dynamo asked. "By listening!"

A hush fell over the crowd.

"When face to face with this young man who had been hastily condemned as a villain, Marvelous Maud did not judge him. Instead, she sought to uncover the nature of his problem. And when he spoke, she listened.

"Now, thanks to Marvelous Maud, we understand young George's actions. Although he has behaved very badly, I propose that we should also recognize his achievements, for he has proved himself to be faster and fleeter than the fastest and fleetest! As such, I think we should also consider the fact that he has much to contribute."

"Hear, hear!" came scattered cries from the audience.

"But wait!" The Daring Dynamo held up his hand. "I would now like to turn your attention to another hero to emerge from today's incident." To Ernie's utter astonishment, The Daring Dynamo was pointing at him!

"It was Extraordinary Ernie," The Daring Dynamo informed the audience, "who clung so bravely to the rope of the balloon as it sailed above the treetops. Was he afraid? Yes!"

Ernie cringed, waiting for the cries of horror and disgust. But The Daring Dynamo wasn't finished.

"Yes, he was afraid. But did that stop him? No! When he saw his partner in trouble, he didn't stop to think of himself—he acted to save his friend. And that, my dear superheroes, is the action of a true hero.

"And so, as our national conference draws to a close for another year, I would ask you to join me in celebrating the superheroes of tomorrow: Extraordinary Ernie and Marvelous Maud! Hip, hip . . ."

"Hooray!" called the crowd.

"And a cheer for the superheroes of Baxter Branch, who are doing such an excellent job of training tomorrow's heroes," cried The Daring Dynamo. "Hip, hip . . ."

"HOORAY!"

EIGHT

There were no arguments in the van on the way back to Baxter that evening. In fact, everyone was remarkably quiet.

Super Whiz was talking in a low voice to Valiant Vera and Amazing Desmond.

"So you're sure my speech was all right?" he asked.

"It was super, Whiz," Desmond assured him. Housecat Woman was stretched out along the back seat again, snoring softly, and Maud was reading in *The Greatest Heroes in History* about the sheep who had piloted the first-ever hot-air balloon.

Ernie, who had the window seat this time, was still thinking over what The Daring Dynamo had said in his closing address, about how heroes weren't necessarily the strongest or fastest or smartest or even bravest people (or animals). Heroes didn't just save people or catch wrongdoers; they also took the time to understand why people became wrongdoers in the first place—which was like saving them in a different way, Ernie supposed. He thought too about what The Daring Dynamo had said about him. Being a hero wasn't about being fearless, as Ernie had always supposed; it was about overcoming your fears. He felt a glow of pleasure as he remembered The Daring Dynamo leading the cheers for him and Maud.

At the roadside restaurant where they stopped for dinner, everyone had extra-cheesy macaroni except Maud, who just had a salad. She had been feeling a little queasy since her hot-air balloon flight.

"You know, Ernie," she confided, as they stretched their legs (and hooves) in the parking lot, "I don't think flying really agrees with sheep. But that's okay. There are lots of ways a sheep can be a hero."

A couple of hours later, the van pulled up at the edge of Mackie's Meadow to let Maud out, and a few minutes later drew to a halt outside Ernie's house. "Bye, Ernie," the superheroes called. "See you tomorrow."

*

The next afternoon, Ernie and Maud arrived at 32 Main Street at the same time for their regular weekly superhero training session.

"I wonder what topic Super Whiz will be speaking about this week," Ernie said.

Maud's answer was smothered by the handle of her straw basket.

As they pushed open the shabby brown door of the headquarters of the Superheroes Society (Baxter Branch), they saw Super Whiz, Valiant Vera, and Amazing Desmond sitting at the large table in the center of the room. Housecat Woman was curled up in her usual armchair.

"Ah, here are our two heroes now," said Super Whiz, sounding much more jovial than usual. "I was just saying to the others that, instead of our usual training session, I think we should share our memories of the conference."

"That means he wants you to say nice things about his speech," Desmond whispered behind his hand.

"Shush, Desmond," said Valiant Vera as she stood up. But she was smiling as she said it. "Since it's a special occasion, I think we should treat ourselves to some lemonade."

As Vera reached for the old chipped mugs lined up on a shelf above the sink, Maud set her basket down on the table. "I have something for you all, Valiant Vera," she said. One by one, she pulled six brand-new mugs from her basket.

Each mug was different, and its owner was obvious.

Ernie's mug was fluorescent green with a gold lightning bolt.

Super Whiz's mug was blue with SW stamped across it in red.

Valiant Vera's mug had a cheerful flower pattern.

Housecat Woman's mug had a striped tail for its handle.

Amazing Desmond's mug had pepperoni shapes stuck all over it.

And there was a plain pink mug that was clearly meant for Maud.

"Wow, Maud!" said Ernie. "This is great!"

"Why, these are all wonderful!" exclaimed Valiant Vera. "Where did you get them, Maud?"

"I made them," said Maud shyly. "My art class did pottery a couple of weeks ago."

Housecat Woman, who had risen from her chair to see what all the fuss was about, sniffed at her mug appreciatively.

"You really are a most remarkable sheep," said Super Whiz thoughtfully, examining his mug in wonder.

Maud beamed.

Amazing Desmond poured lemonade into each of the mugs, then said, "What about a toast then, eh, Whiz?"

For once, Super Whiz didn't snap at Desmond. "Good idea," he said instead. He held up his mug and said, "To Ernie and Maud, the superheroes of tomorrow."

"To Ernie and Maud," the others repeated, holding their mugs aloft.

"So have you decided who to write your school project on?" Maud asked Ernie as they sipped their lemonade. "We certainly met some amazing heroes at the conference, like Stupendous Sue and Lion-hearted Lakmi."

"I have decided," said Ernie. "But it's not someone I met at the conference. It's YOU, Maud."

"Me?" Maud was momentarily speechless. "Me, Ernie? Really?"

"Yes," said Ernie firmly. "The Daring Dynamo called you a hero, and he was right."

"Thanks, Ernie," said Maud sincerely. "And if you like, I could illustrate your project with a self-porpoise."

"That would be marvelous," said Ernie.

About the author

Fearless Frances Watts is the author of *Kisses for Daddy* and *Parsley Rabbit's Book about Books*. She also works as an editor, and as the servant of a lazy cat. Frances likes traveling, cheese, and ducks, and dislikes ferocious dogs and having cold feet. Although her natural superpower has not yet emerged, she did once rescue a horse from a fire.

About the illustrator

Jittery Judy Watson has been a chicken all her life. She has illustrated several books for children, some of them quite terrifying. Her most frightening project so far was drawing the fearsome tiger for the *Aussie Nibble Tim & Tig*. Drawing the pictures for *Extraordinary Ernie & Marvelous Maud* sometimes caused her hand to tremble. This may explain many of the wobbles in her illustrations.

By the way, she is very impressed that Fearless Frances has rescued a horse.

Also available

Ernie & Maud

Extraordinary Ernie & Marvelous Maud

Ernie Eggers is thrilled when he wins a superhero contest and becomes Extraordinary Ernie (after school on Mondays, Tuesdays, and Thursdays, and all day Saturday). But his excitement turns to dismay when he discovers that his sidekick is a sheep. It doesn't take him long to realize, though, that there has never been another sheep quite like Marvelous Maud.

Ernie & Maud

The Middle Sheep

The adventures of Extraordinary Ernie and Marvelous Maud continue . . . but what—or *who*—is making the usually cheerful and dependable Maud so grumpy? And why are she and Ernie arguing all the time? It seems to Ernie that being his sidekick just isn't important to Maud anymore. Then Valiant Vera says that if the two trainee superheroes can't work together, they will be thrown out of the Superheroes Society! Ernie and Maud must learn the value of teamwork (and how to get a sheep out of a tree) before it's too late.